BAD KITTY
Does NOT Like SNOW

NICK BRUEL

For Carina, who really, REALLY does not like snow

Special thanks to Rob Steen

No part of this publication may be reproduced, stored in a retrieval system, or transmitted in any form or by any means, electronic, mechanical, photocopying, recording, or otherwise, without written permission of the publisher. For information regarding permission, write to Roaring Brook Press, a division of Holtzbrinck Publishing Holdings Limited Partnership, 175 Fifth Avenue, New York, NY 10010.

ISBN 978-1-338-27260-4

12 11 10 9   21 22 23 24 25/0

Printed in the U.S.A.   132

First Scholastic printing, December 2017

Book design by Kristie Radwilowicz

SCHOLASTIC INC.

It is snowing.

Kitty has never seen snow.

So Kitty asks the computer,

The computer tells Kitty . . .
Snow is cold.
Snow is wet.
Snow is slippery.
Snow is soft.

Now Kitty is ready for the snow.

The snow is cold.

The snow is wet.

The snow is slippery.

The snow is soft.

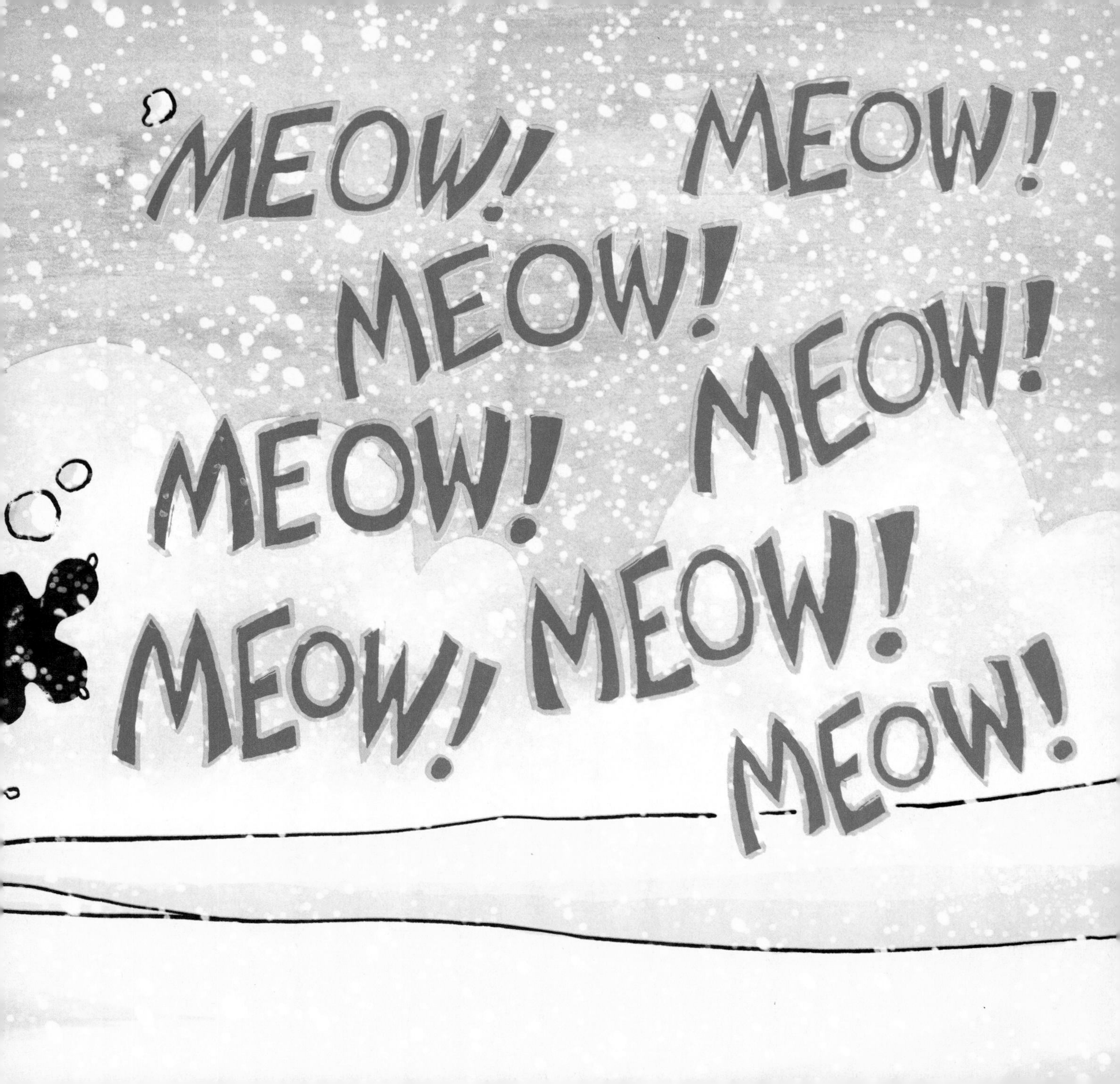
MEOW!
MEOW!
MEOW!
MEOW!
MEOW!
MEOW!
MEOW!
MEOW!

The computer is wrong.

Snow is **VERY** soft!
Snow is **VERY** slippery!
Snow is **VERY** wet!

And snow is **VERY, VERY, VERY, COLD!**

Kitty does not like computers.

Kitty does not like snow.